Story Adaptations by Etta Wilson
Illustrations by Bob Singer
Art Direction by Linda Karl

First published in the UK 1991
by Pipit Press, an imprint of BOXTREE LIMITED,
36 Tavistock Street, London WC2E 7PB

1 3 5 7 9 10 8 6 4 2

© Hanna-Barbera Productions, Inc. 1990

British Library Cataloguing in Publication Data
  Barbera, Hanna
    The Jetsons.
    I. Title
  823.914 [J]
   ISBN 1–85283–079–4

Printed and bound in Hong Kong

PIPIT
PRESS

The Coming of Astro

Jane Jetson greeted Judy and Elroy as they came through the space port from school. Elroy had something with him. "Gee, Mom, guess what followed me home?"

"What in the universe is that — that monster?" asked Jane.

"He's no monster, Mom. His name is Astro, and he's just a baby puppy dog! Can I keep him? Please? Can I?"

"Oh, Mother, can't we? He's so cute," Judy begged.

"Now, you two know how your dad feels about dogs. Well, maybe I'll just call and ask," Jane said.

3

Jane's call on the television phone interrupted another busy day for George. He was pushing buttons at the Spacely Space Sprocket Company as usual.

"We have a request, dear," she said. "Can we have a dog?"

"Not again! I've told you a thousand times — our apartment is no place for a dog. The answer is no!"

George knew the whole family was sore at him when the television phone suddenly went blank.

"Shee! If I don't get a dog, I'll be in the dog house! I'd better use the computer to figure out this one."

"And the answer is . . . of course, we'll get an apartment-approved electronic dog!"

LECTRONIMO

On the way home, George stopped to buy a nuclear-powered, trouble-free, electronic dog! "Lectronimo" was wired to attack anybody wearing a mask because a cat burglar was breaking in space pads all over the galaxy.

SPECIAL TODAY

LECTRONIMO DOGS

FREE DEMONSTRATION

Jane, Judy, and Elroy greeted George with big smiles. It was part of their plan to keep Astro, but George had a surprise for them — Lectronimo!

"Gee, Dad," said Elroy, "what is it? We already have a vacuum cleaner."

In a few seconds, Lectronimo had found Astro. George was not impressed with Elroy's new dog.

"A dog? You call this giraffe a dog? Out! Out he goes!"

Judy had an idea. "Let's have a contest between Lectronimo and Astro."

"Yeah, the best dog stays!" said Elroy.

"I'll be scorekeeper, and there'll be no favorites," George told them.

	LECTRONIMO	ASTRO
FETCHING	1	0
ROLLING OVER	1	0
OVER-EATING	0	1
OBEYING COMMANDS	1	0
BRINGING SLIPPERS	1	0
TOTAL	4	

First Astro raced Lectronimo to find a bone and then to bring George's slippers. No matter what the contest called for, Lectronimo was too fast every time. Astro had lost.

George agreed to let Astro stay for the night, but tomorrow he was out!

"Goodnight, Astro," sniffed Elroy.

The Jetsons—and Astro—were sound asleep when the cat burglar opened the window.

"I'll clean out the place and be gone before — "

BARK! BARK! BARK!

"Oh no, it's one of those nuclear-powered dogs! Help! Help!"

George got up to check the noise and ran straight into the cat burglar — or the cat burglar ran into him!

"Hey, what's going on? Who are YOU?" George asked.

"Here, pal," said the burglar, "you wear the mask!"

BARK! BARK! BARK!

"Good boy, Lectronimo! Go get him!" said George.

BARK! BARK! BARK!

"Not me! I'm not the cat burglar! Help! Help!"

"Don't worry, Dad!" Elroy saw a big chance for Astro to prove himself. "Hey, Astro, wake up! There's a burglar in the house!"

When Astro heard the word "burglar" he started running
— away from the burglar. But the burglar was running away
from Lectronimo.
CRASH!

"Yippee, he did it!" Elroy cried. "Astro captured the burglar!"

Jane and Judy were awake by this time, and George was standing at the door with a policeman.

"This masked guy was trying to sneak in here, folks."

"He's my husband, officer," Jane said. "That electronic dog thought he was a burglar."

"Yeah, my dog Astro captured the real burglar," said Elroy.

"Gee, Dad, everything worked out swell. Can we keep Astro?" asked Judy.

"Yeah, yeah, but don't let him think he's the only hero around here!"

The Flying Suit

Spacely Sprockets is the home of big business where big wheels wheel and deal. Mr. Spacely has just gotten a call from the head of Cogswell Cosmic Cogs, Mr. Cogswell himself.

"Hi there, Spacely. Did you accept my offer? When do we merge?" Cogswell asked.

"The first Sunday that comes in the middle of the week! You can't take over Spacely Sprockets, Cogswell. You're bluffing!"

"Not at all, Spacely! Our research boys have a big new breakthrough. You'd better sell out now."

"Don't hold your breath!" Spacely yelled.

Back at Cogswell Cosmic Cogs, it was time to test the great new breakthrough — a flying suit!

"Why, it looks like an ordinary suit! Is this a gag, Moonstone?" asked Cogswell.

"Oh, no, Mr. Cogswell! With this suit on, Harlan can fly like a bird! The X-1500 flying suit obeys the slightest command of anyone who wears it."

"Fantastic, Moonstone! We're geniuses! Now take the suit to the cleaners. We want it looking fresh for the Board of Directors meeting tomorrow."

"Hey, Herb, I need a rush job on this suit," Harlan said to the man at the cleaners.

"Sure thing. It only takes fifteen seconds with the new high speed sound waves."

"Great! I'll be right back for it."

On the way home George got a call from Jane on his spacemobile car phone. She wanted him to stop at the cleaners.

"Hi, Herb. Mrs. Jetson said I should pick up my suit."

"Sure thing. Here it is."

"Thanks, Herb. Put it on my bill."

"Gee, that suit looks a lot like the one Harlan brought in," Herb said to himself as George was leaving.

When George arrived at the Jetsons' sky pad, Elroy was busy splitting atoms again!

"Hi, Dad. Want to be the first to try my new anti-gravity wrist watch?"

"Not now, Elroy. I gotta change my suit." George thought the clean suit had shrunk a little.

"Please, Dad, try it. Then you can fly around the room."

24

"Okay, okay." George agreed to go along with the joke. "Anti-gravity watches — what a — Hey! I'm flying! Yow-ee! Elroy, you're a genius!"

Jane and Judy couldn't believe their eyes!

"I gotta show Spacely," said George. "He'll make me a vice president. We'll be rich!"

Mr. Spacely was shocked to see George flying by his window! "Jetson! What's going on?" Spacely barked.

"My son Elroy invented this anti-gravity watch, sir. Just put it on your wrist and you can fly!"

"Really?"

"Absolutely! Want to join me in a flight around the building?" asked George.

"You know, Jetson, old pal, I've always thought you ought to be a vice president. Maybe even get a raise. I'd like to see Cogswell top this!"

At Cosmic Cogs it was time to demonstrate the X-1500 suit for the Board. Cogswell promised them a smooth, fast, quiet flight.

"But, Mr. Cogswell, it doesn't work!" Harlan said.

"Don't give me that! Now make like a bird, will you!"

"HELP!"

"I can't believe it!" said Cogswell. "The flying suit has bombed!"

Harlan took the suit back to the cleaners, but there was no hurry this time.

"Hey, this is Mr. Jetson's suit," said Herb. "I'd better get over there with it right away."

George changed suits as soon as Herb came. He wanted to look nice when Mr. Spacely demonstrated Elroy's anti-gravity watch for his Board of Directors.

George buckled on the watch, opened the window, and started to fly off.

"HELP! HELP!"

George, what happened?" Jane asked.

"This anti-gravity watch isn't working! Boy, this was the shortest vice presidency in history!"

When George arrived at the plant, the Board was ready to see Spacely fly.

"Don't do it, Mr. Spacely," George begged. "Don't do it!"

"Be quiet, Jetson! Now watch me, ladies and gentlemen. I put on the watch and Geronimo!"

"Well, Jetson, without that watch, it means the end of Spacely Sprockets. Cogswell can buy this company!" Mr. Spacely was ready to give up.

But Mr. Cogswell didn't need Spacely Spockets any longer. When Harlan brought the X-1500 suit back from the cleaners, Cogswell told him to throw it out the window.

It was soon picked up by the window washer.

"Hey, nothing like a new suit to give a guy a lift!" the man said.

On his way home, George made a big decision.

"No more get rich schemes for me! If I never see people fly, it'll be too soon for me!"

A Date with Jet Screamer

It's almost dinner time at the Jetsons', and George has zoomed in from another hard day of pushing buttons at the Spacely Sprocket Company.

Jane greeted him as he came through the space port.

"Hello, honey. Bad day at the office?"

"Yeah, these three-hour days are killing me," George said. "Hey, what's going on here?"

"Judy's friends are having a meeting of the Jet Screamer Fan Club.He's on TV."

"Not Jet Screamer again!" George exploded. "I will not put up with that noise!"

"But, George, Judy has to listen to you when you play your drums," Jane said.

"That's different. I play music on the drums. Now I want quiet!"

After the house was clear and quiet again, George went to have a little talk with Judy. She was busy doing homework, or so George thought.

"Oh, Dad, I'm writing these great song lyrics for the Jet Screamer Song Contest. If my song wins, I get to go out with him on a real date. I can't lose!"

"Listen, young lady, we're stopping everything on Jet Screamer. No more tapes, no more pictures, no more Jet Screamer — period! Now get back to your homework!" George's words were final.

JET SCREAMER
SCREAMS!

Elroy was coming out of the shower and spin-dry cycle when George asked him what he and his friends had been playing that day.

"We were writing messages in secret code, Dad. See?"

George read, "Eep, Opp, Ork, Ah, Ah — in secret code, eh? That means 'Meet me tonight'."

"Dad, that's a secret!"

"Well, it's no secret that your mother will get us if we're late for supper. Come on."

Just before bedtime, Judy asked her mother to mail an envelope for her the next morning. It was addressed to the Jet Screamer Song Writing Contest. George decided to take care of the contest right then. He took out Judy's entry and replaced it with Elroy's secret code message.

"We've got a guaranteed loser!" he told Jane.

One day a few weeks later Judy rushed home to turn on the TV. George tried to tell her that her chances of winning the contest were very slim. Then Jet Screamer appeared on the screen.

"I'd like to sing the winning song written by Miss Judy Jetson. The song is called "EEP, OPP, ORK, AH, AH," which means 'we've got a date tomorrow night, Judy!'"

"Mom, Mom! I won! I won!" Judy cried. "I've got a date with Jet Screamer!"

"Hey, Dad, he knows my secret code," said Elroy.

George couldn't answer either of them. He had fainted in the chair.

When Jet Screamer arrived the next day, he was not alone. Television cameras filled the Jetson's living room. The announcer introduced Jet Screamer himself and Jet's date for the night — Judy Jetson. Then he turned to George. "And how does it feel to be the father of the winner?" "I feel . . . I feel . . . I feel . . ." George was speechless.

But after Judy and Jet left, George started to worry again. "My daughter's going to have a chaperone — whether she likes it or not!" he said to Jane.

Jet and Judy headed for the Fun Pad where Jet sang in the Swivel Lounge every night. George was not far behind them.

At the back door to the Lounge, George found the entrance for the band and a drummer who was willing to take the night off.

Inside Jet Screamer introduced his band members one by one. "And on the drums . . ."

"It's Daddy!" cried Judy. "What's he doing here?"

"He's a fan, baby. And if he can play the drums, I'll make him a star tonight!"

Jet turned to the audience. "Tune in, Swivelers! Have I got a treat for you. A new song by Judy Jetson! And on the boom booms — Space Dust Daddy himself!"

"Who — me?" asked George.

"You can do it, Daddy! Go get 'em!" Judy called.

45

Jane knew it had been a big evening when George and Judy came home.

"George, what's going on?" she asked.

"Baby, Baby, Baby — Ah, Ah, Ah!" George replied.

"Take a look, Mom, at the new president of the Jet Screamer Fan Club!"

"EEP, OPP, ORK, AH, AH!" George sang.

"That means I love you!"